ISLAND OF DOOM

Don't miss these upcoming
CHOOSE YOUR OWN

titles from Bantam Books:

#4
Castle of Darkness

#5
The Halloween Party

CHOOSE YOUR OWN
NIGHTMARE... #3

ISLAND OF DOOM
BY RICHARD BRIGHTFIELD

ILLUSTRATED BY BILL SCHMIDT
An Edward Packard Book

BANTAM BOOKS
NEW YORK · TORONTO · LONDON · SYDNEY · AUCKLAND

RL 4, age 008-012

ISLAND OF DOOM

A Bantam Book/July 1995

CHOOSE YOUR OWN NIGHTMARE™ is a trademark of
Bantam Doubleday Dell Books for Young Readers,
a division of Bantam Doubleday Dell Publishing Group, Inc.
Registered in U.S. Patent and Trademark Office and elsewhere.

Cover and interior illustrations by Bill Schmidt
Cover and interior design by Beverly Leung

ISBN 0-553-48231-9

Published simultaneously in the United States and Canada

Bantam Books are published by Bantam Books, a division of
Bantam Doubleday Dell Publishing Group, Inc. Its trademark,
consisting of the words "Bantam Books" and the portrayal of a
rooster, is Registered in U.S. Patent and Trademark Office and in
other countries. Marca Registrada. Bantam Books, 1540 Broadway,
New York, New York 10036.

PRINTED IN THE UNITED STATES OF AMERICA

OPM   0   9   8   7   6   5   4   3   2   1

ISLAND OF DOOM

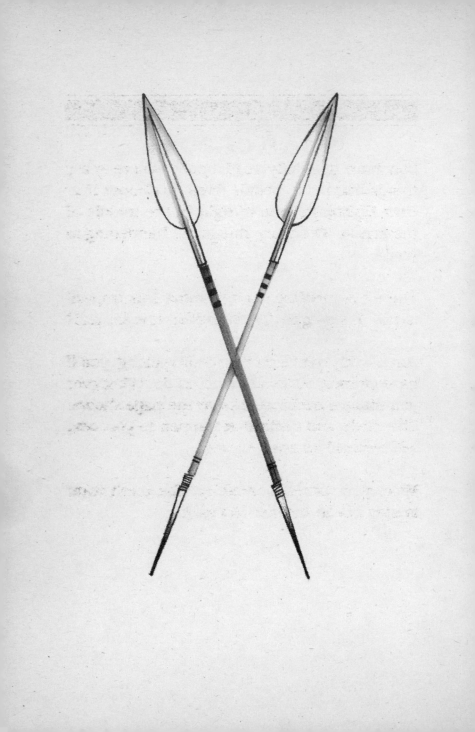

You have probably read books where scary things happen to people. Well, in *Choose Your Own Nightmare,* you're right in the middle of the action. The scary things are happening to you!

There's something strange about this tropical island. It's so quiet. So peaceful. Is it for real?

Fortunately, while you're reading along, you'll have chances to decide what to do. Whenever you make a decision, turn to the page shown. The thrills and chills that happen to you next will depend on your choices.

Make your choices carefully. You don't want to stay out in the sun too long. . . .

You are *really* excited. This year, instead of taking the same old boring vacation you always do, you and your family are flying to Alura, a small island in the Caribbean Sea. You know it's going to be beautiful—white sandy beaches, cool blue ocean, palm trees blowing in the wind—just like the pictures in the travel brochures you've studied. As you look around the plane, you wonder why there are only three other passengers besides you, your mom and dad, and your sister, Betsy. The plane has at least thirty seats, but most of them are empty.

"I guess Alura is not very popular," your father says, looking around. "Anyway, we got a terrific deal on this trip, and at the height of the tourist season at that. It must be the best-kept secret in the Caribbean!"

You nibble on a peanut and look out the window as the plane makes its descent toward Alura. It doesn't look too inviting from the air. It's shaped like a huge dog bone and seems to be covered with thick, dark vegetation. A few tiny beaches appear here and there.

Turn to page 2.

2

Within minutes the plane lands, and you and your family as well as the three other passengers—an elderly couple and their middle-aged daughter—get off. The plane doesn't connect with the terminal. Instead, you have to walk down a tiny set of stairs outside, like someone in an old movie.

The airport looks deserted. Gusts of wind blow dust devils of sand across the landing strip. A deathly silence hangs over the place as everyone stands there waiting. After a few minutes a porter comes out of the seedy-looking terminal. He is wearing a broad-brimmed straw hat and white pajamas—at least they look like pajamas. He is pushing a small rusted hand truck for your baggage.

"The hotel van will be here soon," he says, tipping his hat.

"I hope the hotel is in better shape than the airport," you whisper to Betsy.

"Yeah, me too," she says, wrinkling her nose.

Go on to the next page.

After you have waited a long time, a dilapidated pink minivan finally chugs up to the front of the building. All of you climb aboard, and the van goes off, bouncing along a sandy road toward the hotel.

The Hotel Alura turns out to be a large, five-story structure that has also seen better days. The pink stucco on the outside is in serious need of repainting. Some of the windows are boarded up. Two tall towers, several stories higher than the hotel, flank its front entrance.

"There must be a lot of rooms in this place, but I don't see any other tourists," you say, as you all walk into the lobby.

"They must all be down at the beach, dear," your mother says, putting her tote bag on the floor. "That's why people come here."

"That's where I want to go too," Betsy says.

"All in good time," your father says. "Let's get settled in first. There's still plenty of daylight left."

Turn to page 4.

4

There's only one employee at the check-in desk. He introduces himself as Miguel and tells you that he doubles as desk clerk and bellhop. He helps you carry your bags to a suite of rooms on the first floor, not far from the lobby. The rooms are pretty big, but not at all what you'd pictured. The bedspreads are clean but worn. A broken ceiling fan spins slowly. You peer out a large picture window and see a glimpse of blue ocean. It doesn't take you long to put on your swimsuit, smear on sunscreen, and grab a towel.

"Just a minute," your dad says, as you and Betsy start out the door of your room. He's busy trying to get the air conditioner to work. "You two can go to the beach ahead of us, but no swimming unless there's a lifeguard on duty. And stay near the lifeguard stand."

"Sure thing, Dad," you say. You and Betsy head for the front door of the hotel.

Go on to the next page.

"Which way to the beach?" you ask Miguel, who is now behind the front desk.

"The van that brought you from the airport will take you. It's too rocky for you to walk there. The van'll be back in a few minutes," he tells you.

You and Betsy stand there waiting.

"Not many people here at the hotel," you say.

"We expect a few more to arrive this afternoon," Miguel says. "And then a band—they'll liven things up."

"That still leaves a lot of empty rooms," you say, pointing to all the room keys hanging on the wall.

"I know," Miguel says. Then, after a long pause, during which he seems to be trying to decide if he should tell you something, he adds, "It's because of the ghosts."

"Ghosts?" Betsy repeats.

Turn to page 65.

6

"A fish?"

"It looks larger than a fish. And it has tentacles!" Betsy says.

"An octopus?" you ask.

"Maybe," she says, wringing her hands.

"Do you think we should—" you start to say.

At the same moment, a terrible commotion erupts behind you in the tunnel. You can hear something screaming and thrashing around, as well as growls and tearing sounds.

"What is that!" Betsy exclaims.

Turn to page 48.

"Quick! I've got it open. Let's get out of here!" you say. "Before they come back!"

You slip through the gate and creep back the way you came.

"Please don't let them see us. Please don't let them see us," you say under your breath.

Ahead of you, up the beach, you see torches moving about. They seem to be float-ing back and forth, then around in a circle.

"Now *those* look like ghosts!" Betsy says worriedly. "But the torches look real!"

"They're pretty far away," you say. "We could keep going up the beach until we get close. Maybe they can help us."

"Help us? No way!" Betsy says. "We should circle around through the jungle out of sight. I don't want to get too near those ghosts or lights or whatever they are."

If you keep going up the beach, turn to page 23.

If you decide to slip into the jungle and circle around, turn to page 10.

8

You are about to start down when you see a line of lights moving in the forest. The lights are coming toward you. They seem to be floating through the air.

"Betsy, do you see what I see?"

"Ghosts! Ghosts of the Locomas!"

The lights are moving closer, growing brighter. Now you can make out ghostly robed figures carrying torches. They are chanting to the slow, rhythmic beat of drums.

"We'd better get down to the ground and hide in the woods," you whisper. "We don't want them to catch us up here."

"I don't think there's time," Betsy says.

She's right. The first of the ghosts has already reached the clearing beneath you.

Turn to page 35.

You start along the path. The air is really hot now. As you walk you realize that the path is getting wider and the flowers and plants seem to be getting bigger. Some of them are shaped like mouths, and some are covered with long thorns, while others have several rows of spikes, like gigantic combs.

"Those flowers are beautiful," you say, pointing to one that looks like a hibiscus. "But they look like they're ready to grab something. They look dangerous."

Turn to page 77.

"We'd better hide in the jungle," you say. "We don't want to be captured again!"

"That's for sure," Betsy says.

You and Betsy crawl into the bushes at the edge of the beach. There's not much light. You lie there for a little while.

"Let's go in deeper," you say.

"In this darkness?" Betsy says.

"Look," you say, pointing behind you. "The sunlight is breaking through the trees in spots. I bet there's a path there."

The going isn't easy. You keep tripping over roots and bumping into trees. At first you keep stopping to pick interesting-looking leaves. But after a while, you get tired of it. Thorns scratch your arms and legs, while insects buzz around your head, stopping only to land and bite your ears, neck, or any place they find tasty.

"C'mon," Betsy says, pulling your arm. "You've dillydallied so long it's getting dark. And we don't even know where we are!"

Turn to page 15.

It's even worse than the one in the temple chamber itself.

"Maybe we could get out this way," you say.

"What a smell," Betsy says, holding her nose.

"It's that or climbing up to the window," you say.

Betsy is fighting back her tears. "All right," she cries. "You decide!"

If you decide to try to climb to the window, turn to page 81.

If you decide to explore the stairway below the trapdoor, turn to page 64.

You go over to where she is picking a piece of wood up off the ground. It's an old, weather-beaten sign. You can barely make out the faded lettering. It says H TEL ALURA THI WA , and ends in an arrow.

"Which way was it pointing?" you ask Betsy.

"In that direction," she says, pointing.

"The jungle really looks thick that way," you say. "It seems to thin out in the other direction. There could have been a trail there at one time."

"Maybe," Betsy says. "But that's the opposite direction from where the sign was pointing. I'm sure."

If you go the way the sign was pointing,
turn to page 26.

If you go the other way,
turn to page 68.

The door of the temple is open a tiny bit. You peek inside, but the opening isn't wide enough to see much. You put your fingers in the crack and try to widen it. The door gives way and opens. It's dark inside, with only a faint light coming from the window high up in the dome.

You stop. "Do we really have to do this?" you ask your sister.

"Just a quick look," she says. "If we see a ghost, we'll run out."

Turn to page 70.

14

They force you and Betsy to go with them up the beach. Then they turn down a path that leads to a large bamboo cage. They prod you and Betsy inside with their spears and close the barred gate behind you. One of them shoves a thick pole across the gate and latches it in place. Then they walk over to a small clearing, where there are several bamboo huts.

"Who are these people?" Betsy whispers, frightened.

"I don't know," you whisper back. "But I'd guess they're the ghosts of the Locomas—the ones Miguel was telling us about."

Turn to page 25.

Finally you do reach a path. Your eyes are now used to the dim light, and you manage to hurry along. After an hour of walking, you end up at a huge tree trunk. The path stops there and starts on the other side.

"*Now* what do we do?" Betsy asks.

"I guess we might as well rest here, at the base of this tree," you suggest.

The two of you lie on the soft ground and try to sleep. But the darkness around you is full of sounds. Some are those of birds or insects, but there are also a few deep growls! Sometimes you hear an animal screaming with fear. You feel like screaming yourself! It's a long time before you fall asleep.

You wake up with a start during the night. A pair of yellow eyes is staring at you in the darkness. After a while, the eyes go away.

Turn to page 60.

16

You and Betsy run down a dark trail that leads off the beach in pursuit of the lizard. Overhead, huge leaves, dripping with moisture, block out the sunlight. In no time at all, you are surrounded by clouds of huge mosquitoes. Soon your arms and legs are covered with bites. "This is awful!" Betsy says.

"Let's go back," you say. But then you see a clearing up ahead. You and Betsy dash the last hundred feet to it.

In the center of the large clearing is a white, dome-shaped structure. It looks like a one-eyed human skull! The arched door in the front forms its mouth, and the single half-round window over it the eye.

"Are you thinking what I'm thinking?" Betsy asks.

"A temple built by the Locomas, the people that Miguel told us about," you say. "We'd better get out of here fast. Their ghosts are probably all over the place."

Turn to page 40.

The ride to the beach is pretty short. When you get there, you see the three passengers from the plane huddled under a large blue-and-white-striped umbrella. Two young couples are sunbathing nearby. The twin towers of the hotel rise above the forest skyline in the distance behind you. The beach looks pretty long—but it's only a short distance to the water.

Fortunately, there is a lifeguard, but you see a sign hanging from his small tower that reads: WARNING! JELLYFISH IN THE WATER TODAY. You notice that there is no one swimming.

"What a bummer," you say. "I'm not going in an ocean full of jellyfish."

"I guess the only thing we can do is just sit here on the sand for a while," Betsy says. She starts to spread out her big orange beach towel.

Turn to page 33.

You don't have to look. The sun is suddenly blotted out by a thundercloud. A minute later, a strong wind comes up, followed by a hard, driving rain.

"Get us to shore!" Betsy screams. "Quick!"

"I can't row against this tide alone—it's too strong!" you yell. "Besides, you've got an oar. You help!"

"Okay, okay," Betsy says, her voice slightly shaky.

"All right," you say calmly. "You take one oar and I'll take the other. Maybe the two of us . . ."

You and Betsy sit side by side, rowing as hard as you can. But the rain is so heavy, you can't even see where to go. Waves batter the boat, and blinding spray flies in your face.

Suddenly a huge wave washes over you. You and Betsy find yourselves in the water, choking and clinging to the side of the boat. Good thing you both took that swimming course at the Y.

Turn to page 41.

20

You're running so fast that you're not watching where you're going. Somehow you get off the path. Soon the ground starts to squish under your feet. It gets harder to keep going. Your feet begin to sink into the muck.

"We're heading into a swamp," you call out, still running.

"We can't turn back!" Betsy says. "They'll kill us!"

A short distance farther on, you find yourself wading in dark, murky water up to your knees. You step into a sinkhole and disappear under the water. You fight your way back to the surface, sputtering and gasping. Betsy reaches over and helps pull you back to the shallower part.

"At least it's not quicksand," you say, gulping.

"They'll have a harder time following us in here," Betsy says. Her face is red from running.

"I'm glad there's *something* good about this," you say, trying to make a joke.

Turn to page 75.

"This is funny," Betsy says. "The bunches of bananas are upside down."

"I guess they grow this way," you say, picking several of them off one of the stalks. You hand a couple to Betsy and start peeling one for yourself. You don't really like bananas, but you have no choice. Then you push on through the brush.

Soon you come out into a wide clearing. You and Betsy run over and see a wide path beyond it lined with exotic flowers and plants on both sides.

"It's beautiful!" Betsy exclaims. She bends down to smell a small pink flower.

"I've never seen anything like it," you tell her.

"Maybe you should pick some for your collection," she suggests.

"No," you tell her. "I've got enough."

Turn to page 9.

"Hello!" you call out. The sound echoes through the chamber. It is answered by another scream, this time muffled and far away, as if the person screaming were being carried off by some terrible beast.

"What should we do?" Betsy asks. Her body is trembling.

"I don't know," you say, your knees shaking with fright. "We'd better go back up the stairs."

You are about to do just that when you hear the trapdoor above you slap shut with a terrible bang.

"The w-wind probably blew it shut," you stammer.

"Or *something* pushed it shut—maybe the ghosts of the Locomas!" Betsy says.

You glare at Betsy in the darkness. "Whose bright idea was it to come in here?" you say.

"I know—I'm sorry," Betsy tells you. "I never wanted to run into the Locomas!"

Turn to page 30.

"Let's keep going up the beach," you say.

"Well . . . okay," Betsy says. "But I don't like this."

"Listen," you tell her, "we'll stay next to the jungle. We can always jump into the bushes if we have to."

You and Betsy move silently up the beach. The surf sparkles under the setting sun. You can hear the sound of the waves as they wash up on the sand.

As you get closer to the lights, you start to hear chanting and the rhythmic beating of drums. Suddenly the lights start in your direction. You can see now that the torches are carried in the hands of the same group of Locomas that captured you earlier.

"Quick, into the bushes!" you whisper to Betsy.

Turn to page 50.

You go over to the edge of the beach and begin looking for interesting leaves. You find a few growing on the bushes there. Happily, you pluck them off. Sitting down under a tree out of the hot sun, you examine them. Betsy is out on the beach collecting shells. Suddenly she runs over, all excited.

"Look over there, bobbing in the surf!" she says, pointing off to the left.

"It could be a rowboat," you say. "Let's go see." You carefully put the leaves in your fanny pack. Then you jump up and run across the beach.

A small boat is making its way toward the shore. Each wave brings it in a bit closer, then washes it back out. You run into the surf and grab it on the next wave. There's a pair of oars in the bottom.

"Watch out!" Betsy screams.

You turn to see a large wave coming at you.

Clunk! The rowboat bangs into your leg. Somehow you grab hold of it and limp to shore.

Turn to page 69.

"They don't seem like ghosts to me," Betsy says, eyeing them. "They seem like real people! Do you think there still could be Locomas alive today?"

"Miguel said they died out seven hundred years ago," you say, sitting down.

"Maybe he's wrong," Betsy says nervously. "They might still be around—and planning to eat us!"

"No!" you say. "We're just imagining all of this. It's a bad dream, and we'll wake up soon."

"I've been pinching myself, but I can't wake up," Betsy says. "And besides, it's too hot to be a dream!"

You watch as the men talk and argue with each other. You see a few more men appear. For a while, everyone stares at you, talking in hushed whispers. Then they seem to lose interest in you. The men lounge around, talking and sharpening their spears.

Turn to page 55.

You and Betsy head in the direction she indicates.

"We're still in a fix, but at least it's daylight," you say. "We can find a trail."

"How about just going in the direction of the sun?" Betsy says. "After all, we're on an island. If we keep going in one direction, we should reach the beach somewhere."

"Okay, let's try it," you say. The two of you start off.

"I'm hungry," Betsy says. "We could be having French toast at the hotel," she moans.

"Maybe there are some wild fruits growing around here. Isn't that a banana tree over there?" you say.

In fact there are several small banana trees, about ten feet tall, a short distance away. You and Betsy walk over to them.

Turn to page 21.

"This is much better," Betsy says. "Let's swim the rest of the way."

"Good idea," you say, splashing around and heading toward the hotel. The water feels cool and refreshing, and wakes you up.

Just when you're starting to relax, something attacks you! It feels as though a million jellyfish have wrapped themselves around your body, including your head.

"Ahhh!" you scream, as one of them sucks on your mouth. You frantically swim toward the beach, trying to pull them off. Now something even larger grabs you. You fight it desperately—you can't let this giant jellyfish kill you. You can't!

Turn to page 45.

"There's the hotel!" Betsy shrieks. She's totally exhausted, and so are you. You can't run any farther. Gasping, you fall down on the beach. You're sure the jaguar will kill you. Any moment now, you'll be pounced on by the beast. But nothing happens. Slowly, you lift your head. The jaguar has disappeared.

Then you see your parents. They are sitting a hundred yards away on beach chairs, calmly sipping tall glasses of tropical fruit juice with little umbrellas in them.

"Oh, there you are," they call over, as you and Betsy stumble toward them. "We were starting to worry about you."

The End

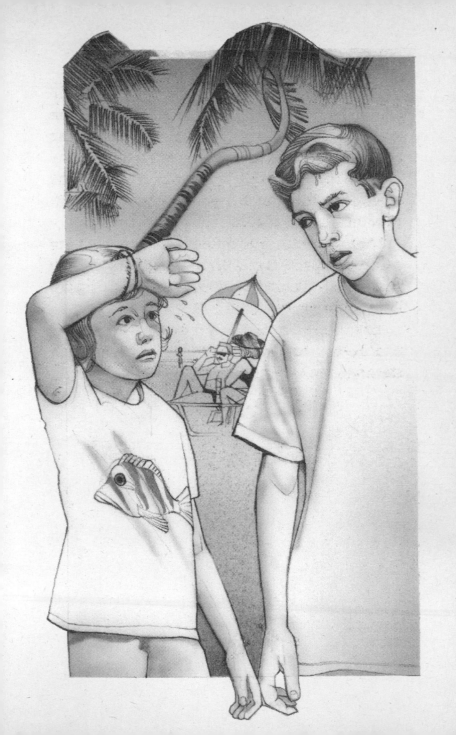

30

Both of you stand there in terror for a few minutes, not speaking. Gradually, as your eyes get used to the darkness, you can see a very faint light coming from an arched doorway on the other side of the chamber. A slight breeze blows from that direction. You and Betsy feel your way along the wall, sloshing along in the ankle-deep water over to the doorway.

"This is the entrance to a tunnel," you say.

"I wonder where it goes," Betsy says.

"There's only one way to find out," you say. You start into the tunnel, with Betsy right behind you. It's still almost pitch-dark, but the floor is now dry. The tunnel curves to the left, and soon you can see light up ahead.

Turn to page 74.

"What'll we do?" Betsy asks in a panic. "They'll think we broke into their office."

You look out through the window in the door. "Two men are out there, heading this way," you say. "I don't like their looks."

There's a door on the other side of the office. Maybe it's a closet.

"Let's hide in there until we find out who they are," Betsy says, pointing to the door. "Maybe they'll only stay a few minutes. Then we can call for help."

You and Betsy run into the closet and close the door. Inside, it is lit by a single dim lightbulb on the ceiling.

But it's not really a closet—it's more like a small storeroom. There are shelves full of large cardboard boxes on one side and spears and shields stacked up on the other. At the back of the storeroom is another door. You open it and see a stairway going down into darkness.

You go back to the door to the office and put your ear to it, listening as the two men come in.

Turn to page 71.

32

"Ugh! This is creepy. And I don't see my lizard," Betsy says. "Let's get out of here."

Suddenly you feel a strong wind blowing through the room. The door to the outside slams shut.

You run back and try to open it. There are no latches or door handles. You push on the door as hard as you can. It doesn't budge. You and Betsy push together. No luck.

You're trapped! The only light comes from the window high up near the roof. Betsy clutches your arm. "I'm scared!" she exclaims.

"We'll find a way out," you say.

"How?" she says, her voice shaking. "I don't see any other doors. The walls are solid except for that window way up there."

Turn to page 57.

"Let's go up the beach," you say after sitting for a while. "Maybe I can find some leaves." Collecting leaves is one of your favorite hobbies. Alura must have lots of interesting trees and plants, you think.

Betsy looks doubtful. "You and your leaves! Dad said to stay near the lifeguard stand," she says.

"That's only if we go in the water."

"Well . . . okay," Betsy says. "I'll race you." She starts running, with you after her.

Finally you both stop, out of breath.

"This part of the beach looks just about the same as where we were," you say. "Except here there *really* aren't any people."

Turn to page 24.

34

"What was that?" the second man says, looking over in your direction.

"There's somebody in the bushes over there," the first man says. "Quick! A reward for whoever catches him, dead or alive—preferably dead!"

All the "Locomas" jump up with their spears and rush in your direction. You and Betsy plunge back into the jungle. You can hear the pursuing "Locomas" crashing through the underbrush behind you.

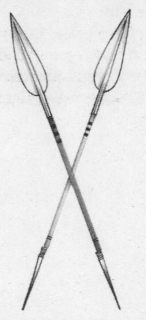

Turn to page 20.

You and Betsy lie flat on the window ledge, hoping you won't be seen. Trying not to move, you peek over the edge. The door of the temple slides open by itself. The figures chant to the rhythm of the drums as they float in.

You shift your position to try to see what's going on. Some of the ghosts are dragging large urns to the center of the chamber. You can't see the urns too well from your high perch, but they look as though they are covered with dried blood.

One of the figures, the only Locoma wearing a robe and elaborate headdress, floats to the front of the altar and raises his arms. Your guess is that he's the high priest of this group.

Turn to page 56.

36

"How about over there?" you say, pointing. "There are some creases in the stone."

You use the last of your strength to reach the smooth, rocky face of the cliff. You grab one of the slight indentations in the stone and painfully pull yourself out of the water. Betsy, still in the water, holds on to another crease in the rock further down.

You try to climb higher, but Betsy was right —there aren't any footholds. Breathing hard, you pull yourself up to a slight crease in the rock, but you can't hold on. You slip off the face of the cliff and back into the sea.

Betsy manages to get almost as high as you did. Then she falls off, plunging back into the water. "It's no use," she says, coughing. "We'll have to keep going along the cliff until we find a better place to climb up."

Turn to page 58.

A silvery lizard, about the size of a house cat, with red and purple scales up its back, is standing just outside the foliage next to the beach. As Betsy starts toward it to get a better look, it scampers back into the woods.

"It went along that path over there," Betsy says. "Let's follow it."

"Maybe we should stay on the beach," you say, thinking of your parents.

"Oh, come on!" Betsy says. "You can find some leaves to collect."

*If you decide to follow the lizard,
turn to page 16.*

*If you decide to continue up the beach,
turn to page 62.*

38

"All right," you say. "Knock on the door."

"Here goes." Betsy steps up to the door and knocks lightly. There's no answer.

"Knock harder," you say, giving it a solid rap yourself.

There is still no answer. You turn the door-knob—the door's unlocked, and you open it partway. "Hello! Is anyone here?"

"Let's go in," Betsy says. "Maybe there's a telephone. We can call for help."

"Why not?" you say. You open the door all the way and step inside.

You're standing in an office of some kind, with several desks, file cabinets, and tele-phones. The desks are piled with papers, as if people have just been working there.

"What number should we call?" Betsy says.

"We know the emergency number to call back home, but that's probably no good here," you say.

"Try it anyway," Betsy says.

"Okay, I'll—" You stop yourself as you hear voices outside.

Turn to page 31.

You take a bite out of one of the large purple fruits. "This is good," you say. The juice dribbles down your chin.

Betsy is trying one of the orange-red fruits. "Yeah. It's delicious," she says, picking a big one. Picking them seems to release a strong fragrance into the air.

As you stand there eating, thousands of mosquitoes come out of nowhere and form a cloud around you and Betsy. They seem to be attracted by the scent of the fruits. The mosquitoes all attack at once. Soon you and Betsy are both covered from head to toe with new bites.

Turn to page 63.

40

"I'm sure they only come out at night," Betsy says. "If they're even real. You can search for some leaves while I look at that door." It's carved with strange-looking figures.

"Okay," you say, examining a small green plant.

Suddenly Betsy lets out a scream and jumps back. "Look at those carvings!" she says. "This one shows a man cutting out someone's heart with a knife! Another man has cut off someone's arm and is eating it! Ughh!"

"Miguel told us about that too," you say, looking at the door yourself. "The Locomas were cannibals. This must show how they ate each other. Now can we get out of here?" Your knees are shaking a bit.

"In a minute," Betsy says. "I just want to take a quick look inside. My lizard may be in there."

"You can't be serious," you say.

"Don't be a scaredy-cat," Betsy says.

If you go inside, turn to page 13.

If not, turn to page 72.

Then, as quickly as it came, the storm passes. The waters grow calm. The beach is only a few yards away!

You let go of the boat and wade ashore. The surf tosses the boat up on the beach behind you. You and Betsy plunk down, exhausted, on the sand.

"We'd better get back to the lifeguard tower," Betsy says. "Mom and Dad may be worried about us."

The two of you start along the shore. Your T-shirts are dripping—but it's so hot you're sure they'll dry fast.

"This doesn't look right," you say, after you've gone a short distance. "The people are gone—even the lifeguard tower is gone."

"Maybe the storm carried us a long way and we didn't realize it," Betsy says. "We'll just have to walk until we get back to where the people are." You continue to trudge along, the soft sand squishing underneath your feet.

Suddenly Betsy stops and points off to the left. "Look at that animal!" she exclaims. "I've never seen anything like it."

Turn to page 37.

"I've got to have them!" you shout, scrambling around trying to pick up some of the leaves. "They're perfect for my collection." But each time you try to grab one, a gust of wind blows it away. It's really frustrating. Soon all your leaves are swirling around you in a whirlwind.

"Ouch!" says Betsy, as a spark from one of the skulls lands on her wrist.

"Just one minute more," you say, lunging forward to grab a leaf. It blows out of your grasp.

Seconds later, the leaves expand to human size and burst into flame before your eyes. Betsy grabs hold of you. "What's going on?" she cries in a panic. "What kind of leaves are they?"

You are both huddled in a ring of fire, unable to get out. The flames now form a circle of dancing, fiery figures—the ghosts of the Locomas! And they are gradually closing in on you!

The End

"Maybe someone is spying on us!" the other says.

"Whoever it is, we've got to take care of him," the first man says. "He's in the store-room."

You grab Betsy by the hand and pull her through the door leading to the staircase.

You and Betsy dash down the stairs, trying not to slip and fall. Somehow you make it to the bottom and enter a dark tunnel.

At the same moment, the two men appear at the top of the stairs with a flashlight. The beam cuts down through the darkness.

"There are two of them! We've got to stop them!" you hear.

There is a flash from the top of the stairs. The sound of a gunshot echoes through the tunnel.

"Ahh!" screams Betsy, grabbing your arm.

The bullet pings on the wall where you were standing a second before. You dash around a bend before your pursuer can get off another shot.

Turn to page 80.

Then you realize it's not a giant jellyfish. It's a lifeguard, trying to remove a *small* jellyfish from your face.

"Look, it's all right," he's saying, his hand on your back. "It's only a small one. And it didn't even sting you."

You look at what he has in his hand: a jellyfish the size of a small tomato. You feel completely humiliated, especially when you see several other kids on the beach—including Betsy—laughing at you.

"Hey, aren't you two the missing kids?" the lifeguard asks you.

You and Betsy nod.

"I'll go call your parents. I have a feeling you two are in big trouble."

The End

"You call yourselves Locomas! Ha! You couldn't scare anybody," he is saying. "We're paying you big money to scare off all the tourists, and there are still two dozen of them at the hotel."

"As long as there are *any* customers at the Hotel Alura," the other man says, "it's going to stay in business. Once it closes, we'll have the whole island to ourselves and we can dig up the buried treasure we know is here."

"It cost a lot of money to build that phony Temple of the Locomas," the first man goes on. "We need to recoup our investment. We will, and then some. All of you will get your share. But first we have to get all of the tourists off the island. It's important that no one knows what we're doing. The government would come and confiscate our money in a second if—"

Suddenly Betsy sneezes.

Turn to page 34.

You continue down. Reaching the bottom of the stairway, you step into cold water a foot deep. As you let go of the wall, your feet slip out from under you again, this time throwing you facedown in the dark, murky water.

"Yuck!" you say, spitting out some of the awful-tasting water. "I think I'm going to be sick."

You try to stand up and slip a few more times before you finally crawl on your hands and knees back to the wall. You manage to pull yourself up on its slimy surface.

Betsy is almost to the bottom of the stairs, holding on tightly to the wall. She takes the final step down and sinks up to her ankles in the water.

"Ughh!" she cries out.

Suddenly her cry is answered by a terrible, bloodcurdling scream from not far away. It echoes for a few seconds in the dark underground vault.

Then all is silent again—except for the pitter-patter of drops falling from the ceiling.

Turn to page 22.

"I don't even want to think about it," you say. "We better dive in quick, octopus or no octopus."

You take a deep breath and plunge in, followed by Betsy. You level out several feet under the water and breaststroke toward the light. It gets brighter as you swim toward it. Fortunately a strong current is carrying you along.

Suddenly something grabs your leg. There's a dark shape below you. Betsy? No! Long, scaly tentacles reach up. One of them seizes your ankle. It's pulling you down. Betsy is swimming above and behind you. You motion frantically to her for help. She reaches down and grabs you by the arm, then starts swimming as hard as she can. At the same time, you kick at the tentacle with your other foot. The beast lets go and you and Betsy shoot upward.

Turn to page 52.

You decide to check out the path first. "It may be an easier way to get back to the beach," you say.

You and Betsy start walking. After a short distance, both of you stop in your tracks.

"I can't believe what I'm seeing up ahead," you say.

"It must be left over from Halloween," Betsy says.

Lined up on both sides of the path, spaced a few feet apart, are long poles, spears really, each with a human skull rammed onto the top. In between are blackened, burned-out torches stuck in the ground.

This is no Halloween joke. "I—I think we'd better turn back now," you stammer.

"Do you think these skulls have anything to do with the ghosts of the Locomas?" Betsy asks.

"I don't know, but—" you start to say. Then you see an interesting plant growing at the base of the skull poles. It has leaves shaped like little people. Each leaf even has two brown spots for eyes.

Turn to page 84.

Both of you slip into the thick foliage at the edge of the beach. You crouch there, shaking with fear and breathing hard as the group of Locomas march by not more than a dozen yards away, their torches throwing ghostly shadows through the trees around you.

You wait until they've gone a good distance back up the beach before you dare to whisper to Betsy.

"I don't know if they'll come back this way," you say. "But we'd better lie low for a while."

"Okay," says Betsy. Together you make a hiding spot out of leaves and branches. You both slide down underneath and fall asleep.

A bright rising sun wakes you up in the morning. You can't believe you slept the whole night there. Your parents must be really worried. Carefully you look out onto the beach. It's deserted in both directions.

Turn to page 73.

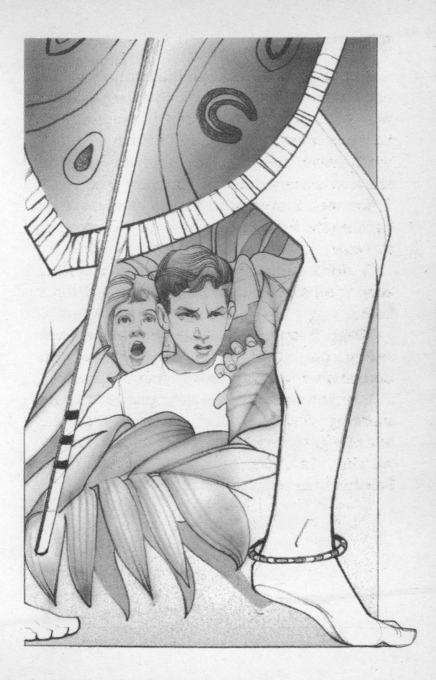

Your heads break the surface of the water. As you both gasp for breath, you look up at the clear sky above. You made it out to the ocean!

"That was close!" Betsy says. "That was an octopus!"

"I'm glad it was a small one," you say, trying not to cry.

You look around. There is no beach, just high cliffs that stretch in both directions.

"*Now* what do we do?" Betsy asks.

"We have to find some way to get ashore," you say. "We may have to climb up one of those cliffs."

"We can't," Betsy says. "They look completely smooth. I don't see any footholds. Nothing!"

Turn to page 36.

"What is it?" Betsy asks.

"Shush!" you whisper, putting your finger on your lips. "I hear voices up ahead."

You and Betsy creep up to the edge of the beach, peeking out carefully from behind the bushes.

You see the gang of Locomas—the ones that locked you in the bamboo cage—sitting on the beach in a big circle. Your eyes widen when you notice two men in straw hats, Hawaiian shirts, and shorts standing in the center. One of them is waving his arms and shouting.

Turn to page 46.

"I hope we can find our way to the hotel," Betsy says. She uses the side of the huge tree to steady herself as she gets to her feet. You brush the leaves off your T-shirt while she puts her hair in a ponytail.

You and Betsy start down the trail. Almost immediately you're joined by swarms of gnats and metallic-green biting flies. Both of you dash down the trail, trying to escape the attacking insects. They swarm around your head, getting into your eyes and mouth.

"Blech!" you say, spitting one out. Soon you can't see where you are going. Blindly running, you lose the trail, crashing through the underbrush at the side.

All of a sudden the insects buzz away, leaving you alone.

"Where are we?" you say, examining an egg-shaped leaf. "We're surrounded by the jungle. I can't tell—"

"Look, over here!" Betsy says. "I just found something."

Turn to page 12.

You move closer to Betsy. You were so caught up in watching the tribe, you almost forgot about her. You can see that she's been crying.

"Look!" she whispers, pointing. Everyone is heading down the beach—and away from you.

"We've got to get out of here," you say. You feel around the edge of the gate and try to grab the pole that holds it shut.

"It's just out of reach," you say, your hand fumbling through the cage.

"You've got to keep trying!" Betsy says. "We've been in here for hours!"

"I am!" you tell her, making sure no one is looking.

After a number of desperate tries, you finally manage to grab the pole and pull it loose.

Turn to page 7.

You shift again, trying to get a better view. Suddenly several bats drop down from the ceiling and fly at your head. One of them wraps itself around your face! "Aghh!" you cry out, trying to tear it loose.

"Manga honga tabla!" the high priest calls out, looking up. He raises his arms toward you as you finally drive off the bats. A loud murmur ripples through the ring of ghosts.

"Manga honga!" the high priest calls out again.

"I—I think he wants us to come down," Betsy says, her voice shaking.

"I guess we'll have to," you say.

Climbing down is even trickier than climbing up was. You are almost to the bottom when you slip and fall the last few feet, landing on the floor in a sitting position. Betsy loses her footing too and lands beside you.

You look up at the high priest ghost towering over you. His face is almost transparent and is framed by a long, white beard. You can see now that his headdress is full of ghostly snakes.

Turn to page 67.

"We might be able to go out through it," you say. "Maybe we could reach it by climbing up one of the statues."

"Let's try looking around for a hidden door or something first," Betsy urges.

You and Betsy start around the inside of the chamber, checking the spaces between the statues. You find that most of them are piled up with bones that look suspiciously like human ones. You are about to give up when you trip over a slight ridge running across the floor.

"I think I've found something," you say, getting down on your hands and knees.

"What is it?" Betsy asks, crouching next to you.

You grip the edge of the ridge with your fingers and pull. A trapdoor springs open. Beneath it you can make out steps. A horrible odor comes up from the darkness below.

Turn to page 11.

You and Betsy tread water as the current carries you along. Suddenly you hear an enormous splash behind you. A gigantic round head, with two huge, evil-looking eyes, has broken out of the water. Long tentacles thrash the surface of the ocean. It's a *giant* octopus!

"Back in the cave! That must have been a baby octopus. This must be its mother!" Betsy shrieks.

"Or its father!" you cry.

Suddenly the giant octopus starts moving rapidly toward you. You and Betsy swim back to the base of the cliff and desperately try to find a foothold—but it's no use! The last thing you remember is the huge tentacles of the octopus wrapping around you. . . .

The End

You huddle at the base of the tree until it gradually begins to get light and a gray mist drifts through the trees around you. Your first thought is how thirsty and hungry you are. You shake Betsy. "It's morning," you say, shivering in your bathing suit and T-shirt.

"What?" Betsy says, her eyes still closed. "Is it time to go to the beach and go swimming? I'll put on my suit and—"

You shake her again. "You've already got your suit on."

She opens her eyes and lets out a cry as she remembers where she is. "I was dreaming we were back in the hotel. Oh, I wish we were." She stretches.

"Well, we're not. We're still stuck in the jungle," you say. "Let's keep following the trail. Maybe it will lead us to the other side of the beach. And maybe the ghosts of the Locomas or whatever they were will be gone in the daylight."

Turn to page 54.

"Quick! Let's go!" you yell, grabbing Betsy's hand and pulling her back through the jungle.

A short time later, you suddenly come out on the beach. There is no one around.

"Yeah! The beach!" Betsy says, jumping up and down.

"C'mon!" you say. "I think the hotel is this way." You and Betsy run up the beach. In the distance you can see the lifeguard tower and several people sitting on the beach near it.

Suddenly several Locomas step out of the underbrush and block your path! You are about to turn and run the other way when you realize that these "Locomas" are not carrying spears—they're carrying musical instruments!

"Don't be afraid," one of them says. "We're only dressed like this for the Polynesian Revue at the hotel. We start in twenty minutes."

You and Betsy sit down on the beach and start to laugh hysterically.

"Hey! I know we look funny," one of them says, "but—"

"No, no. You look great," you say, pulling yourself together. "Just great."

The End

62

"Let's keep going along the beach," you say.

You and Betsy trudge along under the hot sun. In the distance you see a group of men. As you get closer, you notice that they are dressed in green loincloths. Their bronze-colored bodies are painted with spiral patterns of bright yellow and blue. Human bones are tied into their thick, matted hair.

"Draka topa!" one of them commands. There's no time to run! The others rush forward and surround you, pointing long wooden spears at you and Betsy.

"Karooa hanga!" the leader shouts, looking straight at you.

Turn to page 14.

"We better get away from here before we're bitten to death," you say.

You and Betsy run through the jungle. To your relief, you soon find yourself back on the beach! The odor of the fruit seems to follow you—it's now coming out of all your pores. Clouds of gnats and nasty green biting flies descend on you. You and Betsy run back and forth, trying to get rid of the attacking insects.

Then a dark shadow falls over you. You look up and see a monster mosquito overhead. It grabs you with its legs and sticks its baseball-bat-sized stinger into you.

Turn to page 79.

"Let's find out what's down these stairs," you say.

"Do we have to?" Betsy asks. "It looks really yucky down there."

"You can stay up here and wait while I—"

"Oh, no!" Betsy interrupts. "You're not going to leave me up here alone."

"Come on, then," you say, starting down the stairs.

When you have taken several steps, your feet slide out from under you, and you plop down on the stone steps.

"Ow! That hurt!" you say as you struggle back to your feet, trying to hold on to the slimy stone wall at the side of the stairway.

"How are you doing?" you call back to Betsy.

"*I'm* all right," she says. "Keep going!"

Turn to page 47.

"Yes, the ghosts of the Locomas. It's the reason that people have stopped coming here."

"Who are the Locomas?" you ask, shifting your feet nervously.

"It's who they *were,*" Miguel says. "They lived here on Alura over seven hundred years ago."

"What happened to them?" Betsy asks.

"No one really knows. It may have had something to do with their practice of human sacrifice and cannibalism," Miguel says. "I think they sacrificed and ate each other until there weren't any of them left."

"That doesn't sound too bright to me," you mutter.

"They say that the ghosts of the Locomas are still looking for victims," Miguel says.

"I've never heard of ghosts on the beach in the sunshine," Betsy says, as the van rattles up to the front door.

"There's always a first time," Miguel says, a serious look on his face.

Turn to page 17.

"We didn't mean to—" you start to say. But the ghostly priest has turned his back on you. You watch as he floats away, back to the other Locomas.

"Let's get out of here!" Betsy cries. You both start to get up—but you can't. It's as if an invisible force is holding you down.

You watch as the high priest takes out a soft cloth from beneath his robe. *"Troca danto Wamba!"* he says, and begins to polish an urn.

All the other ghosts are floating up and down and moaning excitedly. They too begin to polish urns. They seem to be getting ready for a fresh sacrifice.

The End

You and Betsy decide to go where the jungle is thinning out. A few insects still bother you, but you are almost used to them. The part of your skin that isn't protected by your T-shirt is covered with stings and welts. Maybe the bugs will decide they've gotten all the blood out of you they can.

"We've got to find something to eat soon," Betsy says. "Or I'll faint from hunger."

"I know," you say. "I feel that way too."

After a while, you can hear the sound of surf up ahead.

"We must be close to the beach," you say excitedly. You hurry forward. Suddenly you stop.

Turn to page 53.

"Ow!" you say, sinking down on the sand. It really hurts to walk. "I don't think I can make it back."

"We could row back to the main part of the beach," Betsy suggests.

"Good idea." You struggle to your feet and limp over to the boat. The two of you push it back into the water.

"Watch out for the jellyfish," you say.

"Where?" shrieks Betsy, scrambling into the boat.

You climb in after her. "I didn't see any. I just wanted you to be careful," you say.

You put the oars in the oarlocks and start to row. It's not easy. There's a riptide, carrying you out.

"I think we should go closer to shore," Betsy says.

"I'm trying to," you say. "This current is fierce!" The waves seem to be getting bigger.

"We'd better do something," Betsy says, biting her lip. "Look at those clouds."

Turn to page 18.

Betsy steps inside, with you right behind her. Your eyes gradually become accustomed to the dim light. The whole place has a rancid, unpleasant odor. You're in a large, circular space. The wall is lined with huge stone statues. They seem to be twisting and turning—dancing or in pain, it's hard to tell which. Their tall bodies are covered with red stains and their eyes look gouged out rather than carved. They remind you of pictures you've seen of gargoyles carved on ancient buildings. In the center of the temple is an altar held up by the statue of a crouching jaguar.

Turn to page 32.

"My plan is working," one of them says. "The phony Locomas and the scary tapes are doing their job."

"Yeah, they sure are," the other one says.

"When we've scared off all the tourists, the Hotel Alura will go bankrupt," the first man says. "Then we'll be free to dig up the whole island without interference."

"If we only had a good map of the treasure site, it would be a lot easier," says the second man.

"When we have a free hand on the island, then we'll find the treasure, believe me."

"And the money will be ours!" they say together.

"Those guys are crooks," you whisper to Betsy.

She starts to say something but lets out a screech instead as a mouse runs across her foot.

"Shush!" you tell her.

"What was that?" you hear the man in the office shout.

Turn to page 44.

"I want to take a look around the back of this crazy building before we do anything else," you say.

"Well . . . okay," Betsy agrees.

You lead the way around the base of the temple and find what looks like an ordinary door built into the back.

"This door looks a lot different than the one in the front of the temple. That one looks ancient," you say. "This one looks like it was just put in."

"I'll knock and see if anyone is inside," Betsy says.

"No, wait! We'd better be careful. Something fishy is going on around here. There's a paved walkway going back through the trees over there," you say. "Maybe we should see where it goes first."

"I still think we should knock," Betsy says.

---

*If you decide to knock on the door,
turn to page 38.*

*If you decide to follow the paved walkway,
turn to page 49.*

You and Betsy creep out and start moving up the beach. Suddenly Betsy grabs your arm and points. "Look!" she exclaims. "I can see the towers of the hotel above the trees."

"Civilization!" you shout. "We're saved!"

You both run down the beach toward the towers in the now blazing sunlight. After a minute, Betsy stops and sinks down on the sand. "Wait," she says, pulling off her T-shirt. She's wearing a dark blue swimsuit underneath. "The sun is too hot. It's making me dizzy."

"Let's jump in the water," you say hurriedly. You're afraid the Locomas will come back. "That should cool us off."

You help Betsy up, and the two of you stagger into the surf.

Turn to page 27.

74

"I hope this leads to the outside," Betsy says.

No such luck! You enter a cavern, almost completely taken up by a large lake. A narrow ridge, just wide enough to walk on, runs along the side of the lake just above the water. A bright, bluish light is coming from *under* the water on the far side.

"That looks like daylight filtering under the water," you say. "There must be an underwater exit to the outside. We should be able to get out of here by swimming over to it."

"Go ahead," Betsy says. "I'll dive in after you."

You peer down into the clear water. You can see all the way to the silvery pebbles on the bottom—twenty, maybe thirty feet down. You teeter for a moment on the ledge. Then you take a deep breath and start to count to three.

"Hold it a second!" Betsy cries. "There's something moving down there."

Turn to page 6.

Farther on, you come out of the swamp and sink down on the still mushy ground. Little bugs crawl over your legs.

"I give up," you say. "If we don't drown in the swamps, we'll starve to death." To your relief, you don't hear anyone coming.

So far you haven't bothered to look around. When you do, you realize that you are surrounded by fruit trees.

"We won't starve—look at all that fruit!" Betsy exclaims.

Some of the fruits are colored a beautiful orange-red. Others look like oversized plums. Over on the side are the only fruits you recognize. Bananas. Ugh! You hate bananas.

"Do you think the fruits are all right to eat?" Betsy asks. "I mean, I know the bananas are, but—"

"I think it's some kind of overgrown orchard," you say. "They should be edible."

If you eat the bananas, turn to page 86.

If you eat the other fruits, turn to page 39.

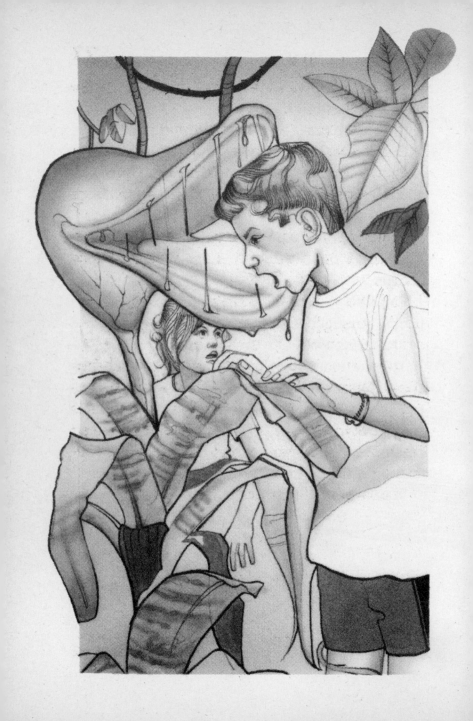

"We don't have to get close to them," Betsy says.

"I know, but—" you start to say.

Suddenly, before your eyes, the vines with long thorns grow quickly along the ground. Their ends weave together, forming a fence around you.

"They've got us trapped!" Betsy exclaims. "We can't push through them with all those thorns."

"Maybe if we just stand still, they'll back up," you suggest.

"I don't think so—they're getting closer!"

You notice that one of the larger, mouth-shaped plants—it's as tall as you are—has appeared in front of the fence. Its open end is turned toward you. It's incredible! You are so fascinated that you don't notice the vine creeping up behind you.

"Look out!" Betsy screams.

Turn to page 85.

78

You and Betsy dash back along the path. As you run you hear a deep growling behind you. Without breaking your stride, you take a quick glance over your shoulder. The large, dark shape of a jaguar, eyes flaming, is hurtling up the path toward you with frightening speed! You do your best to run faster, but everything seems to be trying to slow you down. Long, tangly vines and plants on both sides whip out, trying to trip you, and thorns scratch and cut your skin. A large bird that looks like a hawk swoops down at your head.

"Run faster!" you shout, your feet pounding the forest floor. You hear Betsy gasping for air.

Soon you feel the hot breath of the pursuing beast on the back of your neck. Neither you nor Betsy dares to look back. You both put all your energy into trying to escape.

Suddenly you burst out onto the beach.

Turn to page 28.

"*Yeowww!*" you yell. With a jolt, you bolt up. You're lying on Betsy's big orange beach towel. Betsy is sprawled out next to you.

"Wake up!" Betsy says. "You fell asleep. Somebody just hit you with a Frisbee."

"I'm really sorry," one of the Frisbee players says. "I didn't mean to wake you."

"It's all right," you say. "I was having a really bad dream anyway."

The End

The two of you slosh through a few inches of muddy water on the floor as fast as you can.

The tunnel makes several turns before you come to a heavy, partly open door. You and Betsy squeeze through the opening and slam the door shut. You realize too late that there is no other way out of the small room you are in.

"Now we've got them," you hear one of the men say on the other side of the door.

"We open the door and shoot them, right, Louie?" the other man says.

"No need to do that," the first man says. Then he calls out, *"Hope you enjoy your swim!"*

You hear a lock snap shut on the other side of the door, then laughter going back down the tunnel. Then silence.

"I wonder what he meant by 'Enjoy your swim'?" Betsy says anxiously.

"I don't know, unless—" you start to say. Then you feel water rising up above your ankles—then up to your knees.

Turn to page 82.

"Let's try climbing up to the window," you tell Betsy. "You go first. That way I can catch you if you fall."

Betsy starts climbing up the statue directly beneath the window. She almost slips a couple of times but finally makes it to the right shoulder of the statue.

You follow close behind. As you do, several large, ugly spiders run across your hands and arms. You shudder with fright but keep going. There is no way you can let go!

When you are next to Betsy, you reach up as far as you can and grab hold of the windowsill. Using all your strength, you pull yourself to it, then reach down and help Betsy up.

The two of you sit on the windowsill with your legs dangling down on the outside. The sun has set somewhere beyond the trees. It's almost dark.

"I think we can climb down most of the way, then jump the rest," you say.

Turn to page 8.

"What's happening?" cries Betsy. "Help! Help!" She hops up on an old crate and begins banging on the door.

This must be a bad dream, you think. But the water keeps rising. Now it's up to your waist. Soon it will be up to your chin!

If this is a bad dream, you hope you wake up before the water reaches the ceiling.

Glug, glug, glug!

The End

"Wow," you breathe. "These are great. I've got to take back some of these leaves. Nobody will believe me unless I have them." You bend over and hurriedly start picking the leaves. You want to get as many as you can carry.

Suddenly you hear a rumbling sound, and the ground begins to shake. At the same moment, the torches burst into flame—and the eye sockets of the skulls start spitting out sparks!

You are so surprised that you drop all your leaves.

"Come on, let's run back!" Betsy exclaims.

"I can't just leave all these leaves here. I've got to have some!" you say.

"Forget the leaves!" Betsy cries. "We've got to get out of here!"

If you stop to pick up the leaves,
turn to page 42.

If you run off without the leaves,
turn to page 78.

But it's too late. The vine pushes you off your feet, and you tumble headfirst into the open mouth of the plant. The green lips, strong as steel, snap shut around your feet, holding you tight. A gooey salivalike substance oozes over you.

Betsy is caught too. She's struggling wildly against another of the man-eating plants.

You try to punch the inside of the mouth with your fists. You turn this way and that, struggling to get out.

"Let me go! Open up!" you shriek.

But it's a fight that you both lose. You and Betsy become part of the plants, growing side by side—and bloom at the same time each year.

The End

"I think I'll try the bananas," you say. "Maybe they're better than the ones Mom cuts up to put in our cereal."

You walk over and pluck a ripe banana from one of the trees. You peel back the skin and take a bite.

"This isn't all that bad," you mumble. You finish off the banana and start another one. Of course it helps that you are *really* hungry.

Betsy is also busy eating her share of bananas. "I feel better already," she says happily.

You pick a whole bunch of bananas and sit on the ground eating them. Soon you are surrounded by a pile of banana peels.

"I've had enough," you say. You're beginning to feel a bit queasy. "Let's just sit here for a while and—"

Betsy lets out a cry as she sees a painted face peering out of the bushes. You jump to your feet, at the same time picking up a handful of banana peels. You run over and throw them in the phony Locoma's face. He is so surprised that he falls over backward into a patch of thornbushes.

Turn to page 61.

Laugh TILL YOU Scream!

With each and every one of these scary, creepy, delightfully, frightfully funny books, you'll be dying to go to the *Graveyard School!*

Order any or all of the books in this scary new series by **Tom B. Stone!** Just check off the titles you want, then fill out and mail the order form below.

☐ 0-553-48223-8   **DON'T EAT THE MYSTERY MEAT!** $3.50/$4.50 Can.

☐ 0-553-48224-6   **THE SKELETON ON THE SKATEBOARD** $3.50/$4.50 Can.

☐ 0-553-48225-4   **THE HEADLESS BICYCLE RIDER** $3.50/$4.50 Can.

☐ 0-553-48226-2   **LITTLE PET WEREWOLF** $3.50/$4.50 Can.

☐ 0-553-48227-0   **REVENGE OF THE DINOSAURS** $3.50/$4.50 Can.

BDD
Bantam Doubleday Dell
Books For Young Readers

BDD BOOKS FOR YOUNG READERS
2451 South Wolf Road
Des Plaines, IL 60018

Please send me the items I have checked

above. I am enclosing $_____
(please add $2.50 to cover postage and handling).
Send check or money order, no cash or C.O.D.s please.

NAME _____

ADDRESS _____

CITY _____ STATE _____ ZIP _____

Please allow four to six weeks for delivery.
Prices and availability subject to change without notice.   BFYR 113 2/95